Toot & Puddle
The Mystery of the Disappearing Swing

Based on the teleplay by Stu Krieger
Adapted by Laura F. Marsh

NATIONAL GEOGRAPHIC
Washington, D.C.

For Alyla and Joss -

Just like Toot & Puddle - I hope your lives are filled with many happy adventures both near and far!

Founded in 1888, the National Geographic Society is one of the largest nonprofit scientific and educational organizations
in the world. It reaches more than 285 million people worldwide each month through its official journal, NATIONAL GEOGRAPHIC,
and its four other magazines; the National Geographic Channel; television documentaries; radio programs; films; books;
videos and DVDs; maps; and interactive media. National Geographic has funded more than 8,000 scientific research projects
and supports an education program combating geographic illiteracy.

For more information, please call
1-800-NGS LINE (647-5463) or write to the following address:
NATIONAL GEOGRAPHIC SOCIETY
1145 17th Street N.W., Washington, D.C. 20036-4688 U.S.A.

Visit us online at www.nationalgeographic.com/books
Librarians and teachers, visit us at www.ngchildrensbooks.org

For information about special discounts for bulk purchases, please contact
National Geographic Books Special Sales: ngspecsales@ngs.org.

For rights or permissions inquiries, please contact
National Geographic Books Subsidiary Rights: ngbookrights@ngs.org.

Library of Congress Cataloging-in-Publication Data available from the publisher on request.
Trade Paperback ISBN 978-1-4263-0224-4
Reinforced Library Edition ISBN 978-1-4263-0372-2

Printed in USA

Toot was going on a trip to Easter Island. "The more places you go, the more things you know!" he said.

Sometimes Toot liked to travel and Puddle liked to stay home.

"Puddle and I will have adventures, too!" said Opal, "right here at Pocket Pond."

"Adios!" said Toot.

Opal and Puddle decided to build a tire swing. In the shed, Opal admired a bird feeder that Toot had made. Puddle found an old tire and rope sitting on top of some birdseed.

"How come you tied it with so many knotty knots?" Opal asked.

"So when you go swinging into the water, the rope stays tied to the tree," said Puddle.

Opal had a "bee-yoo-tee-ful" new bathing suit.

"Someone sure looks like they're ready for the tire swing!" said Tulip.

But when they arrived at Pocket Pond, the tire was gone.

By the time Puddle had tied a second tire with his top secret, nobody-can-undo-it, best knot ever, it was too late to swing.

"We'll come back first thing in the morning," Puddle promised.

Just as the sun peeked over the hills, Opal was ready.

"It's time to swing!" she exclaimed. But when they got to Pocket Pond, the tire had disappeared again.

"But, how..." started Opal.

"This is a mystery," said Puddle. "And I intend to solve it."

Puddle searched underwater. He searched all around the rope. Puddle couldn't find clues to the disappearing tire anywhere.

But he did find a postcard from Toot.

"Hola," Puddle read. "I'm making new friends and exploring the mystery of these giant statues. See you soon! Your pal, Toot."

Puddle and Opal went back to searching. Opal heard the "tap, tap, tap" of a woodpecker. But Puddle was not paying attention. He was setting a trap. If somebody was stealing the tires, Puddle was going to find out who.

"You caught yourself!" Opal giggled. Now all they had to do was wait and catch the thief.

Puddle, Opal, and Tulip waited . . .

. . . and waited.

When they woke up, the
tire swing was gone again!
And the trap was still there.

"How can this be?"
Puddle wondered.

Then their friend Otto
trudged up the hill...carrying
three tires.

"You found our swings!"
Opal cried.

Otto pointed at the
woodpecker pecking
at a nearby tree. "That
might explain why they're
disappearing," he said.

"A-ha!" Puddle thought aloud. "The rope was in a bag of birdseed in the shed."

"The woodpecker must have pecked at the birdseed that still stuck to it."

"And his pecking untied the knots and the tires rolled away."

"What can we do?" asked Tulip.
"I know!" Opal said. "I know
how to make everybody happy!"
Opal got the bird feeder and
placed it carefully in the tree.

Everybody was happy.